offside

COUNTERATTACK

M. G. HIGGINS

MINNEAPOLIS

Darby Creek
A division of Lerner Publishing Group, Inc.
241 First Avenue North
Minneapolis, MN 55401 U.S.A.

Website address: www.lernerbooks.com

The images in this book are used with the permission of: Front cover: © Chris Crisman/CORBIS. iStockphoto.com/ Ermin Gutenberger, (stadium lights).

Main body text set in Janson Text 12/17.5.
Typeface provided by Adobe Systems.

Library of Congress Cataloging-in-Publications Data

Higgins, M. G.
Offside / by M. G. Higgins.
p. cm. — (Counterattack)
ISBN 978-1-4677-0305-5 (lib. bdg. : alk. paper)
[1. Soccer—Fiction. 2. East Indian Americans—Fiction.] I. Title.
PZ7.H5349554Of 2013
[Fic]—dc23 2012025235

Manufactured in the United States of America
1 – BP – 12/31/12

FOR BK AND LK.

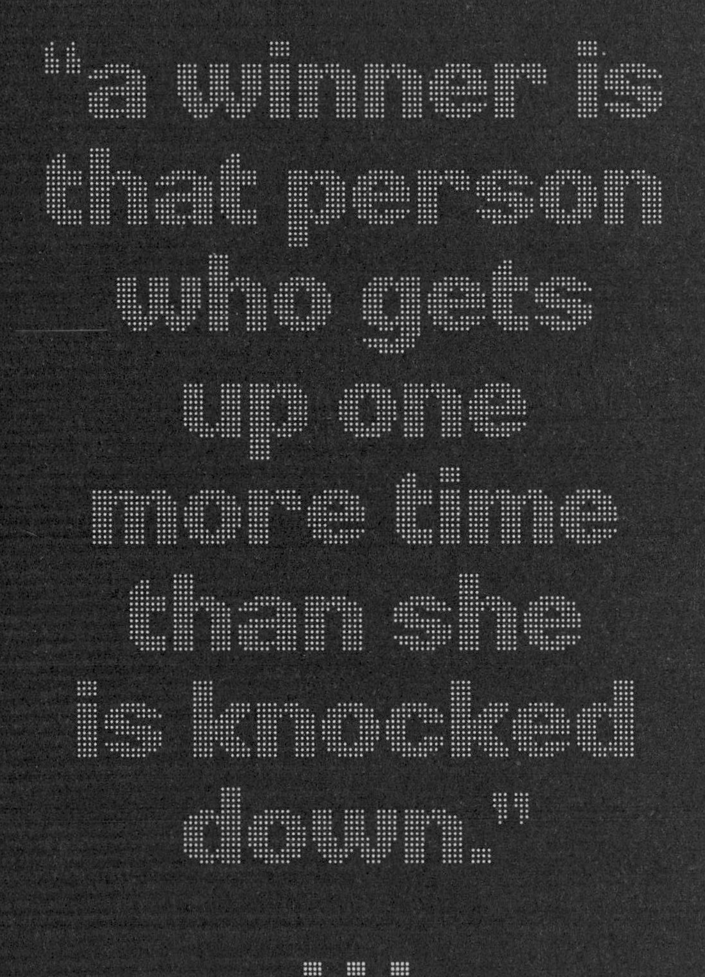
"a winner is
that person
who gets
up one
more time
than she
is knocked
down."

MIA HAMM

chapter 1

Faith turned up the volume on her iPod. But it still couldn't block out the sound of her little brothers screaming in the next bedroom. Between the noise coming through the apartment walls and her old computer software crashing at the worst possible moment, she'd have to stay up all night if she wanted to finish the health report that was due the next day.

Yanking out her earbuds, she yelled, "Will

you please. Shut! Up!"

Like always, Faith instantly felt guilty for shouting. But at least they seemed to quiet down.

She had typed one sentence when Antim screamed, "Give it back!"

"No!" Vijay cried.

"Faith! Vijay isn't being fair!" Antim whined through the wall.

Faith sighed. Sending a silent prayer to the word-processing gods, she clicked Save and strode into her brothers' bedroom. Six-year-old Antim's cheeks were streaked with tears. Vijay, eight, glowered at his younger brother. Faith could see the head of a Lego person in his tight fist. Lego pieces were scattered across the floor.

"Both of you, play fair. And clean up."

"But—"

"No buts! Work it out between yourselves. Just do it *quietly*." Faith glanced at the boys' purple dinosaur clock. It was after ten. "Where's your sister?"

"In the bathroom," Vijay said. He stuck

the Lego man onto a Lego truck and sent it rolling toward Antim.

Faith marched down the hall. The bathroom door was closed. She knocked. "Hamsa?"

No answer.

"Are you trying on Mom's makeup again?"

Faith turned the knob. Locked. "You will never look like Taylor Swift, so stop trying. Wash your face."

"Whatever," came a muffled reply.

Faith shook her head and trudged back to her room. She wanted to send everyone to bed, but she knew it was best to let them wind down on their own.

Five minutes later, Hamsa plopped onto her bed on the other side of their room. Her cheeks were freshly scrubbed, but Faith could still see traces of eyeliner. She smiled to herself, remembering her own fifth-grade makeup phase. She'd hardly worn more than lip gloss since.

Hamsa grabbed her cell phone and started texting.

"Don't you have homework?" Faith asked.

"Finished it."

Faith took a deep breath, ready to lecture her sister on the costs of sending so many text messages. But she returned to her computer. She wasn't Mom. She shouldn't have to do absolutely everything.

⁘ ⁘ ⁘

Faith gave herself two minutes to stretch around in bed and to wish she were still asleep. Then she threw off her covers and locked herself in the bathroom. Having these moments to herself was worth the five-thirty wake-up time. She turned the shower on as hot as she could stand it.

After dressing in her usual school outfit—soccer sweats—she walked into the kitchen. Late-March sunshine just peeked through the curtains. Her mom sat at the table, reading the paper and sipping a cup of coffee. She was still wearing her hospital scrubs.

"Hi, Mom." Faith opened the cupboard

and grabbed a box of cereal.

"Good morning, Astha."

Faith cringed at the sound of her Hindu name. In third grade, Jessie Nichols started calling her "Asthma." It stuck. So in fourth grade, she began using the English translation of *Astha*—faith. Now she preferred it. Her mom preferred tradition.

Without looking up from the paper, her mom said, "Get your health report done?"

"The boys were fighting until quarter after ten. At ten thirty, Hamsa admitted she had a math test today. I was up until midnight helping her study."

"Did you get your report done?" her mom repeated.

"Didn't you hear me?" Faith grabbed milk from the fridge and slammed the door. "When would I have had the chance?"

Her mom looked Faith in the eyes. "Hamsa can do her own work. How will you get into college without good grades?"

Faith shook her head. She refused to have the college argument again. They didn't have the money. She didn't have the grades. She wasn't even one of the Copperheads' starting defenders—her soccer skills were only good enough to keep her on the bench. No scholarship. No college. End of story.

After a few bites of cereal, Faith's stomach clenched and she pushed the bowl away. She really should have finished that report, she thought. Even if she didn't go to college, she at least wanted to graduate high school. Then she'd get a job and her own apartment.

Her mom cleared her throat and said, "I have to cover for Emily this afternoon. So you need to stay home after school."

"What? No! I have a game!" She half-listened as her mom explained how Emily's sick son had an afternoon doctor's appointment. And how Emily had done the same thing for her a few months ago. Blah, blah, blah.

Faith shoved her chair back, carried her bowl to the sink, and dumped out her uneaten cereal. How could her mom go back on their agreement again? For the past three years,

Mom made sure everyone had breakfast and got to school okay. Then she slept until school let out. In return, Faith babysat in the afternoon or evening, giving Mom a couple more hours of sleep. At nine thirty that evening, when Mom left for work, Faith was in charge. In return, Faith got to play soccer. That was all Faith ever asked for.

Faith washed her bowl and set it on the drying rack.

"Astha," her mom said, "your needs can't always come first."

"I'll be home before three," Faith said flatly.

As she was leaving the kitchen, Antim wandered in, dragging a stuffed dinosaur behind him. He grabbed Faith around her legs and mumbled, "Morning."

She patted his head. "You need to get ready for kindergarten, Ant Man."

"Okay." He crawled into his mom's lap.

Faith grabbed the soccer ball wedged underneath her bed. If she left for school now, she'd be an hour early. That was okay. She'd rather be there than stuck at the apartment for the Patel family morning chaos show. As an afterthought, she grabbed the flash drive with her partially written nutrition report. Maybe she'd have time to finish it in the computer lab.

As she passed the hallway's picture gallery, Faith stopped in front of the family photo that included her dad. He was a handsome guy. Smart too. An electrical engineer. Taken in front of their old house, the picture always reminded Faith of her pink bedroom and the nice Fraser suburb. She adjusted her backpack on her shoulder. "Thanks for getting cancer, Dad."

Part of her regretted her sarcasm. A bigger part didn't. She trotted out the door and ran down the apartment steps.

chapter 2

Faith's mom purposely chose an apartment building located between Fraser High and the elementary and middle schools. So what if the building was a total dump in Fraser's worst neighborhood? It was convenient. And inexpensive.

As with every walk to and from school, Faith turned on her iPod. It was an ancient model, but it worked. Faith also plastered on her "don't mess with me" face. But at six thirty A.M., the only people up and about were trash collectors. A garbage truck rumbled by. The guy hanging off the back whistled at her. Faith hunched her shoulders and sped up.

After three blocks, the streets became more residential. Faith slowed her pace. Her jaw slackened. Not only did she feel safer on these blocks, she also liked to admire the lawns and flowers and well-kept houses. Four blocks more and the two-story high school came into view. The doors unlocked at a quarter past seven. That would give her a little time to get her paper done. Otherwise, she was in no hurry for school to start. Following the sidewalk around the main building, then beyond the arts studio, the auto shop, and the gym, she came to the field complex.

The field gate was never locked. Fraser High left it open as a community service or something. Next to the soccer fields was the football stadium and the track. Faith was at the field often enough that she recognized the two adults jogging around the track. While she would have liked the place all to herself, she knew they'd mind their own business.

After setting her backpack and ball on the bleachers, she stretched her quads and started jogging. Her goal was to work off her anger at her mom but not get so sweaty that Andrew Rizzo would hold his nose and fake gag in chem lab.

After four laps, she was pumping some good oxygen into her brain. She'd planned on stopping after a mile to practice dribbling. But it was a perfect morning for running—crisp and dry. She decided one more lap wouldn't make her any smellier than she already was.

Up ahead, at the end of the bleachers, a movement caught her eye. Coach Berg, who led her soccer team, was standing in front of the sports equipment shed.

Faith stopped when she rounded the track close to the shed. In addition to coaching soccer, Berg taught her fifth-period health class. That was when she'd planned on telling him about missing the coming match. But he was gruff to begin with, and he became really grumpy when players missed games.

She figured she might as well get her bad news over with now.

"Hi," she said, slowing as she got close to him.

He twisted around. His dark hair was cut short. He was about six feet tall, probably in his late thirties, and always looked fit. She'd heard someone say he had played on a minor league team for a while.

"Hey, Patel." He inserted a key into a padlock and slid the lock off the clasp. "Good morning for a run."

Faith stepped out of the way as he swung the door open. Then she stood in the doorway as he strode inside. The wooden shed was about the size of Faith's living room, maybe twelve square feet. One side was packed with track equipment and the other with soccer gear. Coach Berg held a clipboard and stared at the soccer side, his forehead wrinkled.

"Coach?" Faith asked.

He looked at her. "Inventory," he said, as though she'd asked what he was doing. "I've been putting it off." He turned back to the mountain of equipment and sighed, shoulders drooping. "I hate paperwork."

Faith had never seen her coach look so overwhelmed.

"Um . . . do you need help?"

"Nah." He stared at his clipboard. "Although it *would* be simpler with two people." He glanced at Faith. "Would I be keeping you from anything?"

She thought about her paper for his class. She wasn't going to finish it in time, anyway. "No."

He handed her the clipboard. "Great. This shouldn't take long. Just write down what I tell you."

She pulled out the pencil that was shoved under the clip.

Faith stayed in the doorway as Coach rummaged through the bags of soccer balls. He mumbled, counting to himself. Then he said, "Okay. Good soccer balls, 38." He pulled up another bag and counted. "Questionable, 4. Completely dead, 5."

The form only included one ball category:

soccer balls. "Um, Coach?" Faith said softly. "I'm not sure where those go."

He strode over and lifted the clipboard closer to his nose. "Oh. If it's not on the list, just write it in the margin. Okay?"

She nodded, and he let the clipboard go before stepping in front of a box of field cones. "Orange disc cones, 60 . . ."

By the time Coach Berg said, "Okay, I think that's it," Faith knew the 8:15 bell would be ringing soon. He stepped next to her and took the clipboard. "Sorry that took so long."

"That's okay." It really hadn't been a problem. They hadn't chitchatted or anything, but she couldn't remember him ever saying more than three words to her. It was nice not feeling invisible. Too bad she had to ruin it with her news.

They walked out of the shed, and he closed the door.

Faith took a deep breath. "I can't play in the game tonight, against Pinecrest."

"Oh?" His eyes met hers.

"I have to babysit."

"Uhhhh-huh. Well . . . okay," he said. "Just don't make it a habit. I count on you for depth." Latching the padlock, he said, "Thanks again." Then he marched in the direction of the gym.

Faith let out a breath of relief. He'd sounded disappointed but not grumpy. As she walked to the bleachers to gather her things, she thought maybe Coach Berg wasn't as gruff as she'd always believed.

chapter 3

At the start of Thursday's practice, all anyone wanted to talk about was the Copperheads' win against Pinecrest the night before.

"Could you believe that striker?" Olivia Cooper said to Caitlyn Novak. The two of them always stood next to each other during drills. Faith was playing across from Caitlyn, paired with her for passing games. Faith wished Coach would let them wear headphones during practice. Instead, she had to imagine music drowning out the chatter from her teammates.

"I know. All she does is talk trash," Olivia said and pushed a pass toward Faith. "I played with her in U11. She's always been like that."

Even when Faith did go to games, she didn't always understand the conversations around her. Most of the Copperheads also played on traveling clubs and went to tournaments and showcases together. They were tight. Since her dad died, Faith's family hadn't been able to afford anything like club fees.

"Cooper! Novak!" Coach yelled. "Focus!" He stormed down the field toward them with his arms crossed. "Okay, chip drills, everyone! I want good backspin and accuracy. We could have used more of each yesterday."

Faith had the ball, so she started first, rolling it under her foot and then jabbing it low across the ground with a sharp, downward motion. The ball rose quickly and flew straight. Caitlyn was able to trap it on her knee without moving more than an inch sideways.

"Nice, Patel," Coach Berg said behind her.

Faith watched him amble down the sideline, his hands clasped thoughtfully behind his back. Should she say thanks? He rarely handed out praise, especially to her.

Whack.

The ball struck Faith right in her face.

Caitlyn snorted. "Wake up, dude!"

Olivia laughed too.

Faith pressed her hand to her nose. She felt like hammering the ball back at Caitlyn. But it *was* her fault. She quickly steadied herself when she saw Coach Berg heading in their direction again. Her next chip went a little wide, but Caitlyn got her head under it. Coach passed by without saying anything.

After practice ended, Caitlyn punched Faith's arm as they walked off the field. "Is your nose okay?"

Faith touched it again. It was tender, but not broken or anything. "I think so."

"Sorry. I couldn't help it if you weren't

watching. You've gotta admit, it was a little funny, though." Her grin practically broke her face.

Olivia jumped up behind Caitlyn, grabbing her in a headlock and rubbing her head with her knuckles.

"Hey!" Caitlyn laughed. "Get off!"

Olivia let go. "Good practice, Cait."

"Want to get some coffee?" Caitlyn asked.

"Nah, can't today," Olivia said.

Since she wasn't usually included in these outings, Faith kept walking.

"Faith?"

Faith stopped and turned.

"Coffee? A chai, perhaps?" Caitlyn raised an eyebrow, smiling. "My treat. To make up for the bonk on your nose."

Faith was taken aback. Was Caitlyn joking? Would her mom mind? She started to open her mouth but had no idea what to say.

Caitlyn rolled her eyes. "Fine. Be rude," she snapped, brushing Faith's shoulder as she walked by.

Faith hung back, balling her hands into

fists. She was so sick of feeling like she was on the fringe of things. She belonged on the team, but she wasn't a starter. She didn't hang out with her teammates because she couldn't speak the club-soccer language. Come to think of it, she didn't have anything in common with anyone at Fraser High. Or at home. Or in the whole city of Fraser.

As Caitlyn and Olivia took off for the locker room, Faith began running around the track, slowly at first, then building to a sprint. After a while, she lost count of the laps, imagining herself somewhere far away. Her lungs burning, her legs turning to mush, she finally slowed to a jog. *I should head home*, she thought. *Mom'll need to nap before she leaves for work.* But Faith couldn't face the noisy, cramped apartment right. The she grabbed a soccer ball and started juggling it from knee to toe and back again. Ten more minutes. Then she'd start walking back.

"Good ball control."

It was Coach Berg. He must have got caught up in something right after practice because he was just then gathering drill cones. "I haven't seen that speed before either."

Faith caught the ball and held it. He must have seen her sprinting around the track.

Throwing the last cone into the box, he said, "Now, you're a junior, right?"

"Yes."

"Have you thought about playing midfield? You seem to have the stamina for it."

Once again, Faith was at a loss for words. Midfield meant running, which she loved. But she'd always thought defense was all she could do. She shook her head.

He hoisted the box of cones in front of him. "You have a nice chip pass too." He nodded slowly. "We may have you in the wrong position. Let's have you scrimmage at mid for a few practices. Depending on how things go next Wednesday, the Lake Valley game, maybe I'll sub you at outside mid." He looked her in the eyes. "What do you think?"

"Um . . . sure. Okay."

He nodded again and left.

For the second time that afternoon, Faith

wondered if she should thank him. But he wasn't doing her a favor. He was just thinking of the team. If she messed up, he'd never mention midfield to her again. Still, it was nice of him to give her a chance. Really nice.

chapter 4

On her walk home, Faith thought about what it would mean to switch positions. She'd always liked defense. But lately she had felt as if she was just going through the motions. The more she thought about playing midfield, the more excited—and nervous—she became. In addition to defending, she'd have to go on the attack. It meant more dribbling—and not getting intercepted. It even meant scoring if she had the chance.

Faith knew mid was a tough position. The Copperhead midfielders, like Madison Wong and Elise Heisel, were constantly moving. They left the field drenched in sweat.

Faith checked the time on her phone. "Crap." She was half an hour late. If she didn't live up to her end of the agreement, it would give her mom an excuse not to live up to hers. She jogged the rest of the way home and flew into the apartment. Everyone was in the kitchen, eating dinner.

"Hi," Faith said, dropping her backpack on the floor. "Sorry I'm late. Practice went long."

Her mom gave her a disapproving look before rising from the table. She rubbed Antim's head. "Be good for your sister."

Antim nodded and shoved a Tater Tot into his mouth. Vijay and Hamsa sat without looking up.

"Have a good nap, Mom." Faith did feel guilty. Working the graveyard shift, her mom never got enough sleep. On days when Faith had practice, it was her job to keep everyone quiet while Mom got a little shut-eye before going to work.

Faith didn't have time to mess around. After dishing up a plateful of food, she glared at her siblings. "I have work to do tonight. You wake up Mom, I kill you. Got it?"

"Got it." Vijay showed her a mouthful of partially chewed potatoes.

"Gross." Faith carried her plate into her room.

Even if Coach Berg subbed her for only a few minutes in the match against Lake Valley, she wanted to make a good impression. Going online, she watched all the YouTube videos she could. She queued up footage of professional teams, like Real Madrid and Barcelona and Manchester United. She'd already watched these games a million times but never while thinking like a midfielder. This time, she studied Kaka's step over and Iniesta's dribbling. Grabbing her ball, she practiced footwork on her bedroom floor.

Faith barely noticed when her mom got dressed and left for work. If Vijay and Antim had beat each other to a pulp, she wouldn't have noticed that either. When Faith collapsed into bed at midnight, Hamsa was sitting on her bed using her cell phone.

"You should be asleep," Faith said, closing her eyes. "What are you doing?"

"Texting axe murderers in Uruguay."

"Okay," Faith mumbled and quickly fell asleep.

chapter 5

The next morning, Faith got to school early and ran laps, trying to build up her stamina. In chemistry, she moved her lab bench away from Andrew Rizzo, hoping he wouldn't notice her post-workout odor.

The Copperheads had a home game that night. For once, Faith didn't mind the time she spent sitting on the bench. It gave her a chance to analyze the midfielders from both teams. She replaced Olivia at defense for the last ten minutes of the game after a rival player kicked Olivia hard in the ankle, but Faith didn't get sent farther up field.

Near the end of the next Monday's practice, Faith trotted out to her usual position for scrimmage.

"Patel," Coach Berg called, "I want you at right midfield today. Lange, you're at center. Wong, take Patel's place at D."

Sophie Lange and Madison eyed each other. Madison shrugged and stepped back.

Faith took a deep breath. She was relieved he hadn't forgotten. She was also anxious about screwing up.

"What's going on?" Caitlyn asked.

Faith shrugged her shoulders bashfully and ran to the right mid spot.

"Okay, let's go!" Coach Berg clapped his hands.

Playing defense wasn't difficult for Faith. It was what she was used to. Offense was the challenge. Faith ran as fast as the other midfielders, but her timing was off. Twice she ended up ahead of the ball. Another time, she lost sight of the ball entirely. It scooted by her across the touchline. She was afraid to keep possession too long, and she passed the ball even when she wasn't being pressured. By the end of the thirty-minute scrimmage, Faith was panting and soaked with sweat.

"Patel," Coach Berg called when she got to the sideline.

She cringed, expecting the worst.

"Nice hustle," he said. "Your field vision can use some work. I know I always harp on passing, but sometimes it's better to dribble and keep the ball for a few touches. Only pass when you're pressured and someone's open."

"Right."

"How do you feel?"

It wasn't the horrible feedback she'd expected. Faith couldn't help grinning. "Okay."

He smiled back and nodded. "Same thing tomorrow."

Out of the corner of her eye, Faith noticed Caitlyn staring at them. Was she scowling?

⁂

The bus for the trip to Lake Valley High left Fraser at four thirty. On game days, Faith's brothers and sister were on their own while Mom took her evening nap. Faith knew her mom kept an ear open and didn't get as much rest as she needed on those days.

Faith grabbed her usual spot on the bus, close to the back. The bus was never crowded, so she didn't have to share a seat. That was fine with her. She didn't want to listen to all the club gossip. She plugged in her earbuds and turned up her iPod as the bus moved out of the lot.

She'd just closed her eyes when she felt someone sit next to her. She looked over. Caitlyn's lips curved into a simpering smile.

Faith pulled out her earbuds.

"So you're moving up in the world," Caitlyn said. "Defense not your thing anymore?"

"There's nothing wrong with defense."

"Then why is Coach moving you to

midfield?"

"He hasn't moved me yet. I like to run. He just thinks it might be a good fit."

Caitlyn nodded. "You know—I saw him smile at you. And I know you were busy looking at him when I bonked you on the nose last week."

Faith stared at Caitlyn. What was she implying?

Caitlyn winked. "It's okay. I won't tell anyone. He's not my type, but he's not a bad-looking guy. For an old dude."

"No! It's not like that!"

Caitlyn tilted her head. "What's that thing Shakespeare wrote about protesting too much?" She paused. "Anyway, I hope it all works out. The good fit and everything." She waved. "Ciao."

Caitlyn walked down the aisle, back to her seat next to Olivia, and whispered in her ear. Olivia turned in her seat and grinned at Faith.

chapter 6

Faith climbed down from the bus with her head lowered, feeling sick to her stomach. Was Caitlyn spreading rumors about her and Coach Berg? It was so unfair. And untrue!

Faith threw her equipment bag onto the end of the bench. Her teammates were milling around and starting to stretch. If Caitlyn was spreading gossip, everyone would be shooting her side-glances. But they were ignoring her, just like always.

Coach Berg stood in front of the bench, jotting something on his clipboard. Feeling self-conscious, Faith quickly looked away. Now she had to worry about Caitlyn reading something into every look and gesture between them. Faith stretched out her right foot and did ankle circles. She could only hope that Caitlyn would get bored and not take her teasing any further. Slowly inhaling and exhaling, Faith tried to clear her head. She wouldn't let Caitlyn throw her off her game.

Faith was on the bench for the start of the match. She watched the flow of the game, the tactics of the Lake Valley players. Their midfielders were fast. Talented too. Was she up to this? She'd only had a few practices at the position. But even with her doubts, she really wanted to give it a try.

As the first half ended, a loud, "Ow!" came from the field.

Fraser High defender Addie Williams was stumbling toward the sideline, limping. Olivia and Caitlyn rushed over and helped her to the bench. She sat and grabbed her calf. "Ow, ow, ow."

Coach Berg walked over to where an athletic trainer had started stretching Addie's leg.

"Bad cramp," Addie said, wincing.

"Well, keep rubbing it out," he said, handing her a Gatorade."

Faith's heart sank as reality set in. He was going to sub her at defense, not midfield. He sometimes used Melody Ramirez at D if Faith wasn't available. But Faith was always his first choice. Her heart sinking, she only half-listened as Coach Berg gave his usual halftime feedback. Afterward, he sat next to the athletic trainer and Addie, who was still wincing and rubbing her leg. Addie nodded in response to whatever question he asked her. Then she shook her head.

No! Faith thought. Addie wasn't retuning to the match.

Coach stood and looked around. "Patel!"

Faith wanted to cry.

Then he shouted, "Ramirez!"

Faith joined Coach and Melody. "Ramirez, go in for Williams. Patel, you're at right mid."

Faith nodded. A relieved, "Thank you," was out of her mouth before she could stop it.

"Don't thank me," he said. "Just do your best. I hope you've been watching the game."

She nodded and trotted onto the field, feeling a ton of bricks on her shoulders. She knew Coach was evaluating her.

Faith's self-consciousness quickly evaporated as she got into the flow of the match. She kept her eyes on the ball and on her opposing midfielder, sprinting up and down the field. At first, the action wasn't coming in their direction. But that suddenly changed when Olivia intercepted a Lake Valley striker. She passed to Madison at center mid. Faith quickly moved out toward the right sideline and sprinted behind the Lake Valley wide back. She watched over her shoulder as Madison dribbled upfield and passed to Elise at left. Elise passed a cross to Dayton Frey, the right forward. But Dayton was out of position, and the ball scooted past her.

Faith was exactly where she needed to be to keep the ball inbounds. She stopped it under her foot. Two defenders were wedging themselves between Faith and Dayton, who hovered close to the goal. Pulling her leg back, Faith chipped the ball over the defenders' heads. It was a perfect lob, but the ball fell from Dayton's chest a little too far in front of her feet. A defender won their foot battle and stole it back for Lake Valley.

Faith sprinted toward the center of the field, covering a Lake Valley midfielder. She tried to stay close, but the girl was quick.

The Lake Valley player faked a move toward the sideline, and Faith followed. Then the girl twisted in the opposite direction. Now in the open, she called to her center midfielder, who passed her the ball. Cursing herself for being tricked, Faith charged. But she was too late to correct her mistake. The girl she should've been covering had already launched the ball to a striker, who sunk the ball into the Copperheads' net.

Amid loud cheers from the Lake Valley players, Faith heard, "Patel!" from the sidelines. Coach was waving her in.

"Crap," she muttered under her panting breath. She'd only played about fifteen minutes. But she understood. With the score tied, Coach wanted his regular players on the field. She trotted to the sideline and stood near Coach Berg, bracing for his feedback. But he was focused on the roster.

Finally, he looked over and said, "I'll talk to you later."

When the match resumed, Coach Berg returned his attention to the field, yelling directions at his players. Faith went back to the end of the bench and plunked down. Coach hadn't sounded angry, but he hadn't sounded happy, either. She'd made a good chip pass, but by not covering her mark, she'd allowed the other team to score.

The game ended in a tie. Coach still hadn't spoken to her. He looked so preoccupied. She figured he wouldn't get around to it that day.

As the Copperheads walked to the bus, Caitlyn suddenly appeared next to Faith. She tugged the back of Faith's hair and chirped, "Midfield fail!"

Faith slapped at Caitlyn's hand. "Leave me alone!"

"Hey!" Coach Berg yelled from behind them.

Caitlyn let go, and the two girls twisted around.

"Are you a third grader, Novak?"

"No, Coach," Caitlyn said.

"Then act your age." He stormed past them.

As soon as he was gone, Caitlyn murmured, "Coach's pet." She puckered her lips at Faith and made wet kissing sounds.

chapter 7

When the bus was a few miles from school, Faith called her mom. The family's old Subaru was in the parking lot when the bus pulled in around nine thirty that night. Faith hung back for a few moments, until most of the girls had grabbed their stuff and stepped out, wanting to avoid another confrontation with Caitlyn.

Her mom started the car before Faith had even shut the door. "It would help if you weren't always the last person off the bus. I don't like leaving the kids alone in the apartment."

"I know." Faith leaned against the headrest. "But it's like ten minutes at the most."

"Can't you sit in the front of the bus?"

Faith turned her head and looked at her mom. She was wearing her scrubs with teddy bears on them. "I'll try."

"Did you win?"

She looked out the windshield again. "No. We tied."

"Did you get to play?"

Faith tapped her armrest. "I'm not getting a soccer scholarship, okay? Colleges don't want benchwarmers with average grades."

"That's not why I asked." Her mom was quiet a moment. "But I do worry about your future." She pulled up in front of the apartment building.

"Yeah, well, I worry about it too." Faith opened her door and jumped out.

Leaning across the front seat, her mom said, "Antim's getting a cold. I sent the boys to bed."

"And you think they're still in bed now?" Faith shook her head. "See ya later." She closed the door, and her mom drove off.

Just as Faith expected, Vijay was sprawled on the living room couch, watching TV. But to her surprise, Antim was still in bed. She pressed her hand to his forehead. He felt warm.

"Someone give you a germ at school, Ant Man?"

He nodded under her hand.

"Can I get you anything?"

He shook his head.

"Okay. Call if you need me."

Faith staggered into her bedroom and belly flopped onto her bed. Hamsa had the laptop propped on her knees. Faith knew she should check what her sister was looking at online, but she didn't have the energy. Glimpses of the botched play churned in her head. She felt Caitlyn yanking on her hair and heard Coach scolding Caitlyn. About to fall asleep, Faith pictured herself running and running. But she wasn't sure if she was running away from something or toward something.

"Faith."

Faith jerked awake. Antim stood next to her bed, sniffling. "I don't feel good."

Faith patted her bed, and he climbed up with her. She held him in her lap until he went to sleep.

∷∷ ∷∷ ∷∷

At school the next day, Faith slogged through morning classes. She hadn't gotten any of her homework done. She'd given up on her nutrition paper since she'd missed last week's deadline. She envied the kids who racked up A's like easy soccer goals.

Fifth period, Faith made sure she got to health class early. She knew Coach Berg didn't like mixing teaching duties with coaching, but she was hoping he'd make an exception. She wanted his feedback on yesterday's game while it was still fresh in his mind. If the news was bad, which it probably was, she wanted to get it over with.

She sat at her desk along the wall, tapping her foot and twiddling her pencil. Coach Berg marched into class late, not giving Faith enough time to talk to him. She sighed and slumped in her seat.

For the next fifty-five minutes, Faith watched Coach Berg lecture with the same intensity that he used in coaching. How in the world could Caitlyn think there was anything going on between them? He was all business, pacing from one side of the classroom to the other. He reminded Faith of a caged tiger. She laughed to herself at the thought of Coach Berg with orange fur and black stripes.

"Patel? You're smiling. Does that mean you know the answer?"

Faith sat up straighter. "What? No."

Coach shook his head. He called on a girl who had her hand raised.

Great. Faith sank back into her seat.

The bell rang. As the classroom emptied, Coach said, "Remember, quiz tomorrow."

Faith grabbed her backpack and slowly approached his desk. He looked up from a paper he was marking. “Hey, Patel.”

“Hey.” She chewed her lip, unsure how to ask about the game.

“I’m glad you stopped by.” He pulled a notebook in front of him and opened it. “I got midterm grade reports this morning. You’re under a C average right now.”

“I am?” She knew she wasn’t doing all of her schoolwork. But she didn’t realize she wasn’t passing.

“You’ll be off the team if you don’t get your grades up. Academic probation.”

“Really?”

“This shouldn’t come as a surprise. I talk about academics at the start of every season.”

Maybe it shouldn’t have been a surprise—but it still shocked her. Off the team? Faith’s legs wobbled. She could feel tears pushing behind her eyes.

Coach Berg must have seen she was upset. He pointed to the empty chair next to his desk. “Have a seat.”

Faith slumped onto the plastic chair.

“Sometimes, staying eligible is just a

matter of turning in missing assignments. Like you didn't turn in your nutrition paper last week. I'll extend your deadline to next Monday. If you get an A on that paper, it will raise your health grade to a B."

Faith nodded, staring at the floor.

"Talk to your other teachers and find out what you're missing. And study! I want you on the team and off the bench."

She met his eyes. "You do?"

"Well, yeah, of course. You made a couple of mistakes yesterday, but that was mostly from lack of experience. We can work on that. You were fast and showed good instincts. I think midfield is your natural position. I notice it's where you sit too." He jutted his chin toward the classroom.

Faith shook her head, confused.

"Your desk against the wall? It's at wide midfield." His eyes twinkled. "That's an unscientific observation, by the way."

She smiled.

He folded his hands. "I remember you said you babysit. Who for?"

"My sister and two brothers. My mother works nights. As a nurse."

"Young kids can be a handful." He nodded thoughtfully. "So you don't play club ball?"

"No. We can't afford it."

A student wandered in for sixth period.

Faith stood and looped her backpack over her shoulder. "I guess I'd better go."

"Don't worry, Faith," he said. "I'm sure you'll get a handle on it. See you at practice."

"Okay."

Faith, she said to herself in the hallway. *He called me Faith.*

Maybe he did care about her as a person. She hadn't felt that understood by anyone in a long time. Faith's footsteps were just a little lighter as she walked to her locker.

chapter 8

"Run closer to the touchline, Patel!"

Coach Berg had given Faith about ten instructions in a row during scrimmage. It was hard to keep track of what she was and wasn't supposed to do. She sprinted up the sideline and then moved into the empty space right of the goal.

"Sheridan!" he yelled at the Copperhead's left forward. "Pass already!"

Lacy Sheridan kept the ball close as she

scanned the field. Faith was the only offensive player open. She could tell Lacy wanted to get the ball to another striker, but they were all covered. Lacy sent up a cross to Faith. Faith ran to meet it. She had a clear view of the goal, but she hesitated.

"Shoot, Patel!" Coach screamed. At the same moment, Nita Ortiz called out, "Faith!" The center forward was sprinting behind Nita. Faith tapped the ball toward her. Nita struck at the net, but Becca blocked it.

Faith shook her head as she ran back down the field. She hadn't made a goal since middle school. She had zero confidence that she could get the ball past the keeper.

Keeping an eye on her zone, Faith moved in to help the defenders. Right behind her ear, she heard a kissing sound and "How's it going, pet?"

Faith shoved her elbow back into Caitlyn's ribs.

"Ow! Hey!"

Before Caitlyn could retaliate, Faith's side got the ball back, and she was running downfield on the attack. Faith was sick of the sneers she'd been getting from Caitlyn lately. But hitting her was stupid, and Faith regretted it. Fighting was a sure way to get kicked off the team. At least Coach hadn't yelled at her—she guessed he hadn't seen what happened.

A few minutes later, Coach blew his whistle and scrimmage ended. "Remember," he announced, "Coach Simmons is subbing in for me tomorrow night. Make me proud. And we're having a Monday match next week, not a Wednesday one."

As players left the field for the locker room, Caitlyn threw death stares at Faith from over Caitlyn's shoulder.

Normally, Faith would have headed straight home. But between her skirmish with Caitlyn and stress over playing midfield, she still had energy to burn. Taking a deep breath, she started jogging. Running also gave her time to review the afternoon's practice. She'd felt a little more comfortable on the field, but not completely comfortable. The longer she played midfield, the less she seemed to understand the position. The strategy was completely different from defense. There were all sorts of patterns to memorize. Maybe the bench *was* the best place for her.

Breathing hard, her legs giving out, Faith finally stopped running. She passed Coach Berg, who was gathering ball bags.

"You know, there's such a thing as too much exercise," he said.

Faith nodded and stopped. She pressed her hands on her hips. Talking to Coach Berg about her misgivings was something she never would have done a week ago. But after their chat in fifth period, she had a feeling he'd understand.

"I'm not sure about playing midfield."

He handed her a bag filled with balls. "Giving up already?"

She hadn't thought about it as giving up. She slowly reached out and took the bag.

He shrugged. "Okay. I'll keep you on defense." He headed toward the equipment shed.

Confused, Faith stood there a moment.

He looked over his shoulder. "That *is* what

you want, right?"

She started following him. "I don't know."

They'd reached the shed. He unlocked the door and opened it. "Look," he said, stepping inside. "It sounds like you've got a lot of responsibilities at home."

Faith followed him in.

He threw the bags he was carrying into the corner and faced her. "Soccer shouldn't add to your stress. If you're going to worry about anything, it should be schoolwork. Academics always trump athletics."

She didn't know what *trump* meant, but she understood what he was saying. "Do *you* think I should stop playing midfield?"

"Based on your overall performance, no. I've already told you, I think you have potential. But it will take time and hard work to get good at it."

Faith took a deep breath, relieved he still thought she had potential. "What kinds of things should I work on?"

"Well, first remember that you won't be playing at all if you don't get your grades up. Striking practice would help. If an opportunity to score is right in front of you, take it. Your dribbling could be a little better—you're not used to going long distances with the ball. Practicing one-on-ones would help." He reached out for the bag of balls she was still holding. "Is that enough?" He smiled.

She smiled in return, meeting his eyes. "Yeah, I think so."

Their fingers touched as she handed the bag to him. He turned and threw the bag on top of the others. She couldn't get over how nice he was being. He was concerned about her grades and her home life. He was giving her all kinds of advice. He didn't need to be so kind. So why was he?

One possible answer sent heat into Faith's face. She scolded herself: *What's wrong with you?* She was glad her skin was dark so Coach Berg wouldn't see her red cheeks.

"Okay," he said, brushing his hands together. "Let's get out of here. Time to go home."

As they stepped outside into the setting sun, Faith saw a flash of movement. A few yards away, someone was trotting away under the bleachers—a tall girl with light brown hair. A girl who looked a lot like Caitlyn.

chapter 9

After dinner, Faith sat in front of her laptop at her desk. Feeling like she'd studied enough for her health quiz, she decided to focus on her nutrition paper. She had to compare five unhealthy snacks with five healthy alternatives. She'd already come up with the foods. Now she had to explain the differences. She'd just typed, "Potato chips are high in oil, calories, and salt," when Vijay walked in and tugged on her sleeve.

"Antim is sick."

"I know he's sick," Faith said. "He has a cold." Antim had stayed home from kindergarten with Mom that day, which meant Mom had gotten even less sleep than usual. She'd gone to bed the second Faith walked through the door.

"Come and see." He tugged on her sleeve again.

Faith sighed before clicking Save and following Vijay to his room. All Antim's covers were thrown off. He squirmed on the bed and mumbled. She felt his forehead. It was way too hot.

"Oh, Antim." She hated to wake her mom, but she had to.

He had a temperature of 103. Faith helped her mom give him Tylenol, popsicles, and a lukewarm bath.

Soon the brother's dino clock reached nine thirty and Mom prepared to leave for work. "Are you sure you'll be okay alone?" she asked.

"I've done this before, remember?" Faith said, more grumpily than she should have.

"Well. Call me if his fever rises. And make sure he drinks plenty of water."

"Okay. Bye, Mom." Faith closed the door behind her.

These were the times Faith hated most. She loved her brothers and sister, but not the responsibility of caring for them. As she walked back to Antim's room, she imagined leaving home again and only being responsible for herself. Coach Berg had seemed to get it when he'd said kids were a handful. Had he also taken care of younger siblings? Was he the oldest in his family?

Between checking on Antim and keeping Vijay from worrying too much, Faith didn't get much done on her report. At this rate, she'd never improve her grades.

By eleven thirty, Antim was sleeping quietly and his fever hadn't risen any higher. She'd check on him again in a few hours. In the meantime, she decided it was safe to go to bed.

But instead of sleeping, Faith lay on her back, completely awake. She'd started thinking about Coach Berg again and why he was being so nice to her. About what she'd wondered in the equipment shed: could he . . . like her? Not as her coach, but in a different way. A *romantic* way.

Faith's cheeks heated up again and she rolled onto her side, digging her fingernails into her palms. The idea was so embarrassing. It was stupid. He was her teacher. He was twenty years older. He was probably even married. Faith couldn't remember—did he wear a ring?

But he'd been smiling and looking at her with such warmth and kindness. She'd never seen him look at other players that way. And he'd defended her against Caitlyn. He *did* treat her differently. He talked to her like he understood her, like she was more than just a student or a soccer player. And he was going out of his way to train her for a new position.

Turning onto her back again, Faith listened to Hamsa's faint snoring across the room. Was it possible?

No. Of course not. She tried to push the thought out of her head.

But as Faith neared sleep, she recalled the faint scent of his cologne in the equipment shed earlier and the touch of his fingers when he took the ball bag. She sighed happily in spite of herself.

⁂ ⁂ ⁂

"Astha. Wake up."

Faith awoke to her mom's gentle shaking. She bolted upright. "What? Is it Antim?"

"No. He's better. You slept through your alarm. I thought you might need the sleep." Her mom stroked Faith's cheek and left.

Sun streamed through Faith's window. She looked at her clock. School started in half an hour. So much for practicing soccer before class or trying to finish homework. She rushed through her shower and breakfast and ran out the door.

Faith barely had time to open her locker before English class started. As she grabbed her textbook, a folded piece of paper fell onto the floor. She picked it up and carried it to class.

Faith landed in her seat just as the bell rang. Mrs. Delsanto began lecturing about the Shakespearean sonnets they were supposed to have read last night. Faith lowered her eyes, hoping she wouldn't get called on to answer a question. The piece of paper was still in her hand. She unfolded it.

The classroom seemed to shrink as she focused on the page. It was a printed-out photo of her and Coach Berg in the equipment shed. It was the moment she'd handed him the mesh bag of balls. They were staring at each other, smiling, their fingers touching. Their faces were so close together, it looked like they were about to kiss.

Faith heard a snicker and quickly folded the page, shoving it into her notebook.

"Is that you?" Jeremy Nyquist whispered over her shoulder. "Who are you with?"

"No one!" she hissed, grateful he hadn't recognized Coach Berg. She wanted to cry.

No, she wanted to die. Caitlyn must have taken the photo. That's why Faith had seen her running under the bleachers the day before.

Faith's heart sank. Who else knew about this?

Moving slowly so she didn't attract Mrs. Delsanto's attention, she pulled her backpack onto her lap. She turned on her phone inside the backpack, hoping to muffle the sound. There was a message waiting, from *caitlove*:

Hey, pet! Enjoying your special treatment? <3 <3 <3

"Faith!" Mrs. Delsanto glared at her. "No phones in class!"

Faith turned it off and dropped her backpack on the floor. Had Olivia seen the picture too? Addie?

The entire team?

chapter 10

As she sat through English, all Faith could think about was confronting Caitlyn. But they didn't have any classes together. The only time Faith might get her alone would be before or after the game that night. But first, Faith had to get through the rest of this horrible day.

As she walked out of English class, it crossed her mind to skip school altogether. But her mom was home. Faith could fake being sick, but that was hard to pull off with a nurse for a mom.

Faith slunk late into every class, right after the bell rang. Keeping her head down, she listened for the snickers and taunts that would tell her if the photo had gone viral at school. To her relief, no one treated her any differently. In other words, they didn't notice her at all.

At lunch, Faith sat at her favorite spot under some trees on the far side of campus. Pulling her backpack onto her lap, she pulled out a PowerBar from the stash she always kept. She also took out the photo. She'd considered tearing it up at least fifty times since her English class. It would be a disaster if it got into anyone else's hands. Both she and Coach Berg would be in huge trouble if school administrators thought something was really going on. He might even lose his job.

She unfolded the sheet of paper.

The image gave her a humiliated, sick feeling. But it also sent a tingle straight to her toes. While she'd been trying to convince herself that Coach Berg's behavior was just teacherly interest, Caitlyn's photo told a different story. Coach looked down at her tenderly, his eyes sparkling. She could still feel their fingers touching. Maybe he'd *chosen* to touch her. Just as he'd *chosen* to hand her the bag in the first place.

Faith shook her head. She didn't know what to believe. As she gently folded the page and returned it to her backpack, she wondered again if Coach had seen it. If he had, what did he think? How would he react when he saw her in class today? Faith's emotions ranged from disgust to jittery anticipation. Since fifth period was right after lunch, she didn't have long to wait.

In the restroom, Faith brushed her hair and applied colored lip gloss, something she didn't normally do. She shook her head as she stared at her reflection. What was she doing? Trying to impress him? She wiped her mouth clean again and strode into health class just as the bell rang.

Coach Berg's eyes briefly met Faith's when he took attendance, but that was it. She took a deep breath. If he'd seen the photo, he would have given her a more meaningful look, she was sure of it. And, as in her morning classes, she didn't notice students peering at her or whispering behind her back.

Clearly, Caitlyn hadn't shared the photo with anyone else. Again, Faith wondered what Caitlyn was up to. Was there something she wanted? Would she use the photo as blackmail? Was she waiting for some perfect moment to ruin Faith's life?

Worrying about Caitlyn soon gave way to thinking about Coach Berg. Faith couldn't help it. Striding back and forth in front of the class, he was so tall and confident. He was the handsome tiger she'd pictured the other day. Try as she might, Faith couldn't look away. She blushed and sighed. She'd never noticed how attractive he was.

As class drew to a close, Faith knew her thoughts were raging out of control. She knew it was wrong, but she started imagining being with him—with Alan. His first name was Alan, wasn't it? She silently laughed at the idea of calling him anything but Coach Berg.

Alan Berg. She wrote his name in her notebook. Then she wrote it again and again.

Alan Berg

Alan Berg

Alan Berg

The bell rang. Faith quickly closed her notebook so no one would see what she'd written. She drew in a breath, suddenly aware how crazy it would look.

What was wrong with her? How could she think about Coach Berg this way? She *was* crazy!

Faith pressed her forehead against her hands and closed her eyes. Her noisy, chattering classmates spiraled around her, sending her stomach twirling. She thought she might cry or throw up. Or both.

"Patel?"

She raised her eyes.

Coach Berg sat at his desk. Everyone else had left.

"You look a little green around the gills," he said. "You okay?"

She lowered her hands and nodded.

"Good. Can we expect you at tonight's match? I want Coach Simmons to have a full crew."

Faith's heart sank. She'd forgotten he wasn't coaching tonight's game. She strained not to show her disappointment.

"I'll make it," she said, beaming.

He paused, still looking at her. "How's the situation at home? Finding time to get your homework done?"

She had the urge to rush behind his desk and hug him. "Kinda."

"Great. So . . . you'll have your nutrition paper turned in next week?"

She nodded.

"Have a good game this afternoon." He lowered his eyes.

Moving slowly, Faith rose and lifted her backpack. She stopped in front of his desk.

He looked up.

"I, uh, was just wondering." She reached

out and touched a pen in his pencil cup. "I was wondering about the name of your cologne?"

His eyes widened a little.

"I need to buy a gift for someone. A guy. A guy friend. And I noticed yours when we were in the equipment shed. It smelled nice."

"Um, I'm not sure. It's something my wife buys for me."

His wife. Oh. Faith lowered her head but stayed rooted to the floor.

"Don't you have a class to go to?" he asked.

She nodded. "See you later." She waved and trotted out the classroom.

In the hallway, just outside the door, Faith leaned against the wall and knocked her fist against her forehead. *What is wrong with me?* she wondered. Taking a deep breath, she straightened up and walked toward math.

She was crushing on her teacher-slash-soccer coach. It didn't get much lamer than that.

chapter 11

Whether having a crush on Coach Berg was lame or not, Faith ran home after school feeling focused. She wanted to work a little more on her nutrition paper before she left for soccer.

Her mom stood at the kitchen sink washing dishes, her shoulders rounded. She looked up when Faith walked in. "Can you finish these?"

"I've got homework. I'll do them later."

"Then will you please sit with Antim?"

Faith rolled her eyes.

"Astha," her mom scolded. "He still has a fever. I'm worried."

"I thought it was just a cold."

Her mom shrugged, her entire body sagging with the effort. "I'm not sure."

Faith sighed. "Fine. You'd better get some sleep." She stepped into the boys' bedroom. Vijay wasn't there. He and Hamsa must still be walking home from elementary school. Antim was curled up on his bed, mumbling softly. His damp hair stuck to his forehead.

"Hey, little Ant Man," Faith murmured.

He didn't open his eyes.

Faith tiptoed to her bedroom, then returned with her laptop and sat on Vijay's bed. The sweeping way the covers were thrown aside, she knew her mom had slept there that day. *Antim is okay*, she told herself. The kids had been sick before. They'd all gotten over it. She opened her Word doc.

"Okay. Carrot sticks instead of potato chips."

⁂ ⁂ ⁂

Faith had wanted to get to the field early to practice—and to talk with Caitlyn. She had to get this photo thing straightened out. But her mom needed the sleep, and Faith left home at the last minute.

As she stretched her hamstrings, Faith noticed the chatter was louder than usual. The laughter had a sharp edge. That night's conference game was against the Midtown High Muddogs, one of Fraser's biggest rivals. The Copperheads were on top of the conference standings, but the Muddogs would tie them with a win tonight. Balding and paunchy Coach Simmons paced in front of the bench, checking his clipboard again and again. Coach Berg must have had something really important going on to miss this match.

Several yards away, Caitlyn stretched her calves. She looked up as if she felt Faith staring. After a quick glare, she looked away. Faith shook her head. What was her problem?

Faith decided she couldn't wait until after the match to find out.

"Three laps!" Coach Simmons yelled.

Instead of running ahead of everyone like she usually did, Faith hung back. She waited until Caitlyn caught up and jogged next to her.

"Hi, pet," Caitlyn said. "How's it going with Coach?"

Faith rolled her eyes. She looked ahead and over her shoulder to make sure they wouldn't be overheard.

"Do you want money or something?" she whispered. "Because I don't have any."

Caitlyn narrowed her eyes. "What are you talking about?"

"You haven't sent that photo to anyone else, have you?"

Caitlyn paused. "Maybe. Maybe not."

"Well, I don't think you have. So what do you want?"

"Maybe I just like watching you squirm."

"Why? Because I hit you with my elbow? I'm sorry."

"Yeah, you should be."

"Okay. I've apologized. Now will you explain why you suddenly hate me so much?"

Caitlyn jogged silently for a few strides, her jaw muscles flexing. Finally, she said, "Coach wouldn't let *me* change positions when I asked him. I don't know what makes you so special." She glared at Faith. "And just for the record, I really *was* asking you to coffee last week. Would it kill you to be friendly once in a while?" She sped up.

Faith slowed her run, wanting to put even more distance between them. What had Caitlyn meant about asking Coach to change positions? And she was accusing *Faith* of being unfriendly? Yeah, Faith kept to herself. But it wasn't like she pushed people away. People pushed *her* away.

Whether she liked being benched or not, starting the match on the sideline gave Faith time to think. She stared at the ground, pondering what Caitlyn had told her. It was true Faith didn't interact much with other players. She could see how someone might see that as being unfriendly. And, she had to admit, when Caitlyn had reached out to her last week, her response had been silence and a dropped jaw. Faith crossed her arms. She had her reasons. It wasn't fair for Caitlyn to judge her so harshly.

Faith steered her train of thought toward the match. The ball was on the Copperheads' side of the field. Caitlyn was crowding a Muddog forward, keeping the forward's back to the goal. Caitlyn was tall and big-boned, and seemed at a glance to move awkwardly. But she was quick and more athletic than she appeared. She was persistent too. She kept on the ball like she was personally offended it was in her zone. Without a view of the net, the Muddog forward had to pass.

Caitlyn had her personal faults, but she was a good soccer player. It suddenly struck Faith: goalkeeper. She bet that was the position Caitlyn had asked Coach Berg if she could play. But of course, Coach had refused to switch her. Unlike Faith, Caitlyn was too valuable to the team as a defender.

The Muddog forwards weren't getting past

Caitlyn. So they started focusing on the other side of the field, running Olivia and Addie ragged. Twenty minutes into the first half, a striker slipped between Olivia and Addie and scored.

"Patel?" Coach Simmons called, looking around the bench.

Faith jumped up.

"Go in for Williams." Then he yelled, "Williams!" He waved at Addie. "Keep it tight out there!" he called to the defenders.

Addie was panting heavily when she slapped Faith's hand coming in. Faith went to her position between Caitlyn and Olivia. She took a deep breath. Since she was a sub, the Muddogs might try to test her early. She'd have to be ready. She glanced at Caitlyn for some reason, wishing she would look back at her. But Caitlyn stared straight ahead, all business.

chapter 12

The Muddogs seized possession as soon as the half started. With the ball at midfield, Faith and the other Copperhead defenders hustled back toward their goal.

A Muddog midfielder passed to one of her strikers. The girl tried to skirt around Caitlyn, who kept herself in front of the ball like a brick wall on cleats. The striker passed to another attacker, who ran to meet the cross in front of Faith. Faith sprinted to intercept the ball before the striker could get there.

Faith had the skills to make the play. An okay play. What was the difference between her and Caitlyn, she wondered as she ran. Passion? Faith didn't have it. That was why she spent most of her time on the bench. It had nothing to do with being at midfield or defense or wherever. It had to do with *desire*—with *wanting* to play her best. She wanted that fierce feeling.

With a surge of urgency, Faith picked up speed and slid into the ball just as the striker pulled back her leg to kick. The ball shot behind the striker. It was a clean tackle, and the ref didn't call a foul. Elise took possession for the Copperheads and drove down the field.

Panting, her adrenalin pumping, Faith sprinted back into position.

"Wow, Faith," Olivia called. "Nice tackle."

"Thanks." Faith felt good, like something had clicked. She glanced over at Caitlyn, who still didn't look at her. Why was she being so stubborn?

Addie returned to the match later in the second half, and Faith headed back to the bench.

⁘ ⁘ ⁘

By game's end, the Copperheads had squeaked out a 3–2 win. Coach Simmons, relieved, couldn't stop congratulating everyone. Faith saw Caitlyn leaving the field with Olivia and Addie. She trotted and caught up with them.

"Hey. Can you talk a minute?"

Caitlyn rolled her eyes but stopped walking.

"See you at Madison's party, Cait," Olivia called.

Caitlyn waved. "Yeah. See ya later." She crossed her arms and stared at Faith. "What?"

Faith suddenly forgot what she was going to say. Madison, a Copperhead midfielder, was having a party. And no one had invited her.

Caitlyn must have seen the disappointment on her face. Her scowl softened. "Um. You can come, if you want. I'm sure Maddie won't care."

"No, that's okay." She cleared her throat. "I just wanted to tell you I'm really sorry about elbowing you. And I'm sorry if I seem unfriendly. I don't mean to be."

"Then why are you?"

Faith shrugged. "I like to keep to myself."

"Ohhh-kay? Personally, I don't get it, but it's a free country."

Without thinking, Faith blurted, "I have to take care of my brothers and sister. My . . . dad died. And my mom works nights. I couldn't go to Madison's party if I wanted to. I couldn't have gone to coffee with you either."

Caitlyn's eyes widened.

Faith sighed. "Sorry."

Caitlyn's shoulders rose and fell as she took deep breath. "I didn't know you had all that stuff going on at home. Can you at least, like, go out on your mom's days off? I mean, she doesn't work seven days a week, does she?"

Faith shook her head. Then she said, "You asked Coach about playing goalie, didn't you?"

Caitlyn frowned. "Good guess, Sherlock. He said we have too many keepers already, and he needed me where I was. The jerk wouldn't even consider it. Oops," she said sarcastically, "Sorry for calling him a *jerk*. I know you're into him."

Faith didn't respond.

Caitlyn's frown deepened. "That doesn't blow half as much as the fact that he seems to like you too." She crossed her arms.

"Caitlyn, seriously—what do you want from me?"

"Nothing."

Faith's eyes widened as it struck her. Caitlyn wasn't jealous because Coach Berg was switching Faith to midfield. She was jealous because he was paying attention to Faith and not her.

"You like Coach Berg!" Faith said. "You're mad at *him*, not me."

Caitlyn pressed her lips together, face flushed, then turned on her heels and marched off.

"Caitlyn."

Faith started to follow but stopped when she heard a familiar horn honking. Looking toward the parking lot, she saw her mom waving at her from the Subaru. Faith trotted to the car, wondering what was going on. She usually walked home if the game ended before eight.

Through the window, she saw Vijay in the front seat. Antim lay in the back, wrapped in a blanket with his head on Hamsa's lap. Faith jumped in, lifting Antim's feet and lowering them onto her legs.

"What's going on?" Faith asked her mom.

"Antim had a seizure. We're going to the hospital."

chapter 13

The ride to the emergency room was silent and grim. So was the wait in the hospital lobby. Her mom vanished with Antim down a corridor while Faith sat with Vijay and Hamsa, who immediately got out her phone and started texting. Faith didn't tell her not to. Vijay sat quietly reading a kid's magazine.

"I think there are toys in that box over there," Faith said.

He shrugged.

She knew they were scared, just like she was. Faith settled into her seat and folded her hands in her lap. She wished she'd grabbed her iPod out of her backpack. She felt like she couldn't take a deep enough breath.

Please, let him be okay, Faith repeated silently over and over. Vijay and Hamsa were too young to remember the endless hours spent in hospital waiting rooms when their father was sick. But Faith remembered. She didn't want to go through that again. She couldn't.

It was an hour later when her mom, hair askew and face flat, trudged down the hallway. Faith thought her heart would stop. She didn't breathe again until she saw her mom slowly smile.

"He's okay. Dr. Effron says he was severely dehydrated. They're giving him an IV, and then we can take him home."

"Can we go see him?" Faith asked, tears pooling in her eyes.

Her mom nodded.

⁂ ⁂ ⁂

Knowing Antim was okay was a huge relief. Faith doted on him over the weekend, reading him stories and filling his old sippy cup with water and juice. But the close call also reminded her just how much looking after her siblings had worn on her. While she'd been stuck in the hospital worrying if Antim was going to live or die, Caitlyn and the other Copperheads were partying. After every game and practice, Faith had to rush home so her mom could sleep or go to work. It was just like she'd told Caitlyn: Faith had no time for friends.

She felt frustrated, angry, and—when she could admit it—guilty. Her mom assured Faith it wasn't her fault Antim had a seizure. But what if it was? What if she'd paid more attention to him, made sure he drank enough water when she was babysitting? Faith wasn't cut out for nannying. She was desperate to leave home. She *had* to graduate and get a job, any kind of job, so she could be on her own.

⁂ ⁂ ⁂

On Saturday, Faith finished her nutrition paper and made up a couple chem assignments too. Sunday night, she sat on her bed reading English homework. She leaned her head against the wall, thinking about apartments. They cost money—especially studios or one bedrooms. More than she'd ever make working at an entry-level job.

She shook her head and looked back at her textbook. *Focus.* While she didn't understand half of what Shakespeare wrote, some of his sonnets did strike her as pretty romantic.

Closing her eyes, Faith thought about Coach Berg . . . Alan. He was a bright spot in her life. The only person who treated her kindly, who seemed to appreciate what she was going through. She wondered what he was doing at that moment. Was it possible he was thinking of her?

Faith jumped up and rummaged through her backpack. She found the printout of Caitlyn's photo and returned with it to her bed. Carefully unfolding it, she studied the image: his fingers touching hers, his tender gaze, his warm smile.

He did like her. She was sure of it.

And she liked him. She had to stop fighting her feelings. So what if he was older, or her teacher?

It suddenly occurred to Faith that Caitlyn had done her a favor by taking the picture. And Faith didn't care who she sent it to. The image simply proved what Faith already knew—that she and Coach Alan Berg were in love.

⁘ ⁘ ⁘

Stuffing her backpack with a change of clothes, Faith left the house Monday morning at six thirty. Alan had told her she needed to work on dribbling and striking to play midfield. She'd decided to practice until she dropped.

When she got to the nice neighborhood on her way to Fraser High, Faith slowed and stopped in front of one of her favorite houses. The white cottage had a picket fence surrounding a neatly mown lawn and yellow rosebushes. Early morning sun glinted off the two front windows framed with blue shutters. Faith wasn't sure why the old-fashioned house appealed to her. It just looked . . . cozy. She imagined cooking Alan breakfast before he headed off to work every morning. Maybe he'd pay her tuition to go to college.

Once at the track, Faith glanced at the equipment shed. Alan wasn't there. With so much to discuss, they needed time alone. Her cheeks warmed as it dawned on her that she and Alan hadn't yet kissed. Maybe it was time they did.

chapter 14

After her morning practice, Faith showered and dressed in the jeans and shirt she'd brought with her. During lunch, she camped out in the restroom. Her mom had given her a makeup kit two Christmases ago. She'd hardly ever used it. But she'd thrown it in her backpack that morning, along with her best clothes.

Leaning over the restroom sink, she gingerly applied some mascara. She used lipstick instead of gloss. After brushing her hair, she tipped the perfume bottle she'd "borrowed" from her mom onto her wrists and neck. Stepping back, Faith hardly recognized the woman in the mirror. She nodded. It was exactly the effect she was going for.

Alan was standing outside the health classroom when Faith arrived, talking to Mr. Cho, one of the social studies teachers. Not wanting to awkwardly wait around, she headed inside to her desk and sat there, heart pounding. Grabbing her textbook and notebook out of her backpack, she listened as Alan and Mr. Cho laughed. The conversation moved briskly but quietly, as the men went back and forth in low voices, and Faith couldn't hear what they said. Finally, Mr. Cho slapped Alan on the back and left. Faith quickly removed the nutrition paper from her notebook. Taking a deep breath, she rose from her desk.

A student rushed into the classroom. "Hey, Coach! There's a fight down the hall!"

"Oh, great," Alan grumbled. He rushed

down the hallway.

Faith slumped back into her seat, tapping her fingers on her desk. Then she straightened up again.

"Alan," she whispered, rehearsing the speech she'd been thinking about all morning. She reached out and touched her notebook as if she were touching his hand. "I know how you feel about me. I feel the same way. I'm ready to—"

Jacob Lane walked in, and Faith stopped talking. As he sat at his desk the next row over, he turned around and did a double take.

"Wow. I didn't recognize you. You look . . . nice."

She lowered her eyes and smiled.

"Kind of heavy on the perfume, though. Sheesh." He waved his hand in front of his nose.

Faith bit her lower lip and remembered her lipstick. She wiped her teeth with her finger.

Class started late. Alan seemed distracted as he took attendance. He didn't even look at her when he called her name. Splitting up the fight must have troubled him. He was a sensitive guy.

When the period ended, Faith stayed at her desk, waiting for the classroom to empty. But the same moment that Faith got to her feet, Sheila Baker stormed back into the classroom waving her quiz in front of his face.

"Why did I only get half credit on my essay answer?" Sheila raged.

Faith sat down again and wiped her damp palms on her thighs. After Alan explained why Sheila's lame essay was hardly worth half credit, the girl left.

They were alone.

Faith jumped up. Her nutrition assignment clutched in her fist, her heart beating in her chest, she trotted to Alan's desk.

"Hi," she said breathlessly.

"Hey, Patel," he said, standing and shuffling papers. "Coach Simmons said you made a nice defensive play Friday. Finish your assignment?"

She handed him the report, her hand trembling. "I . . . I know how you—"

"Yeah, I wanted it today. Great." He set the assignment on a pile of other papers. "See you at tonight's game. Four thirty." He crossed the front of the classroom, heading for the door.

". . . Yeah," she answered, then wandered back to her desk and picked up her backpack. She rolled her shoulders. This wasn't the end of the world. There would be other opportunities to talk. A classroom wasn't very romantic, anyway.

"Hey." Alan was leaning through the doorway, his hand on the doorframe.

He'd come back!

"Um . . . I'm not sure, but I may have a favor to ask you after tonight's game." He grinned sheepishly. "I just want you to know it's okay if you say no."

"I . . . I won't say no."

"Well, no need to answer yet." He slapped the doorframe. "Okay. Later."

chapter 15

Faith ran home after school, her feet barely touching the sidewalk. She flew through the apartment door and hugged her mom. "I love you."

Her mom patted Faith's arm. "I love you too." She pushed Faith away and held her by the shoulders. "Are you on drugs?"

"No! I'm just happy."

Her mom slowly smiled. "That's nice. I'm going to my room."

"Mom," Faith called. "Do you mind if I do stuff on Saturday sometimes when you're off work? Like, go out with friends?"

"Of course not. I wish you would."

"Thanks. Have a good nap." Alan was the *friend* Faith planned to do stuff with. But that afternoon wasn't the time to tell Mom about him.

Antim wandered into the kitchen and wrapped his arms around Faith's legs.

"Hey, Ant Man!" She lifted him up and squeezed him in a bear hug.

"Ow," he whined. "Too tight."

⁂ ⁂ ⁂

Faith got to the field as early as she could. She'd been daydreaming about Alan's favor. Did he want to know if she'd go to dinner with him? Maybe take a trip somewhere? Each scenario she thought of included kissing. Lots and lots of kissing.

Players were already gathering on the field, but she didn't see Alan. The door of the equipment shed was open. She trotted over and peeked inside. He was stepping in between deflated balls and cans of sideline paint, pulling at the goal net.

Her heart flipping, Faith stood behind him. “Hi.”

Alan jumped and turned. “Jeez, Patel. You scared me.” He took a breath. “I’m glad you’re here.”

Faith tilted her chin up, signaling it was all right if he kissed her now.

“Are you okay?” he asked.

She lowered her chin. “Yes.”

“So, that favor? I was hoping I could find *someone*, but no one’s available, so I’m afraid it’s a worst-case scenario.”

“What?”

“I don’t have anyone to watch my boys after the game tonight. And I have to get to the hospital.”

Boys? Hospital? Faith gaped at him.

“Sorry. I’m a little frazzled. Here, take a look.” Alan pulled out his cell phone and pressed a couple of buttons. He held the screen under Faith's nose. In the photo, a dazed but happy-looking woman in a hospital gown held a red-faced infant. "That's little Angelica, just born Friday. And my wife, Jennifer. They're coming home tomorrow."

Then he clicked to a photo of two boys aping for the camera. Faith guessed they were about eight and six. "The older one is David, and the little guy is Jeff," Alan said. "They're great kids, but they think hospital hallways are ice rinks."

Faith looked up. Alan was beaming. Finally, she understood. "You want me to babysit?"

He slid the phone into his pocket. "Just for a couple of hours. With pay, of course. I thought of you because you said you had siblings you take care of. And I know you're responsible. But remember, you can say no."

She hesitated. "I . . . I can't. I have to babysit my brothers and sister. My mom works nights."

Alan hit his forehead. "Oh, that's right! You told me, and I completely forgot." His sheepish grin was back. "I told you, I'm frazzled."

Faith shrugged.

"That's okay, don't worry about it," he said. "I'll go to plan B."

Faith lowered her head and turned to leave.

"Hey, Patel," he said.

Faith stopped without turning.

"If there's an opportunity to use you at midfield tonight, I will."

She nodded but didn't look back.

chapter 16

Faith lumbered to the Copperheads sideline. She should have stretched, jogged, or juggled a soccer ball, *something* to get ready for the match. But why bother? Alan. Coach Berg. Her soccer coach and health teacher—that was all he was.

And he had *three kids*.

She sat on the bench and buried her head in her hands. She started to cry, too devastated to feel ashamed about doing it in public.

The bench bounced as someone sat next to her. "You okay?"

Faith recognized Caitlyn's voice. Without looking up, Faith shook her head. "I just heard Coach has a new baby. Crap." She sat up and wiped her nose with the hem of her jersey. The field was a blur. "He wanted me to watch his sons after the match."

Caitlyn snorted. "He asked you to babysit? Are you freaking kidding me?"

Faith shook her head.

"What a jerk."

"It's okay," Faith said. "He's not a bad person. I just made a mistake. I shouldn't have liked him."

Caitlyn was quiet a second. "Yeah, falling in love with a teacher never turns out well. You'll get over it eventually." She rose to her feet and walked onto the field.

Faith watched as Caitlyn, Olivia, and Addie passed a ball back and forth. Taking a few deep breaths, she got to her feet and positioned herself at an angle between Caitlyn and Olivia. Caitlyn sent a pass her way.

Faith returned to the bench when the match started. The Copperheads were playing the Blue Lake Trojans. It was a team they'd beaten easily earlier in the season. But whether it was because the match was on a Monday night or Coach's head was someplace else—like with his *wife and new baby*—the Copperheads were already down 2–0.

Faith's head wasn't in the game either. *I'm an idiot*, she thought.

She'd misread every one of Coach Berg's kind words and gestures. He wasn't being romantic, he was just showing concern. Caitlyn's photo captured a moment in time that didn't mean anything. Alan—Coach—was trying her at midfield to help the team, not because he was doing Faith some huge favor. And she'd thought he might kiss her that night? Confess his feelings? She wished there were a hole in front of the bench that she could crawl into.

At halftime, the score hadn't changed. It seemed like the threat of a loss hadn't dawned on Coach Berg until the team huddled together. He laid into them.

"I know you're tired! But Monday matches are no different than any other night. You will not lose to this team! You're better than they are."

He waved Faith over.

"Look," he said, "about midfield. If we were ahead, I'd consider it. But not tonight, okay?"

She nodded. It was what she'd expected.

"But Addie needs a break."

"Okay. Great." It surprised Faith how much she wanted to play defense. She felt comfortable there. And it was where she could help the team most right then.

Inspired by Coach's grilling, the Copperheads quickly scored. But soon after the Trojans took possession, they were deep into Copperhead territory again. Caitlyn charged the attacker with the ball. She reached in with her foot to steal, but the forward did a stepover and kept possession.

"Crap!" Caitlyn yelled as the forward dribbled toward the goal.

But Faith had already shifted to back her up. She was focused on the ball in front of her but aware of the net behind her back. The net was the lake. She would not let the ball drown. The Trojan forward must have seen the resolve on Faith's face—she pulled up short. Caitlyn rushed in alongside Faith, double-teaming the charging Trojan. Under pressure, the forward made a weak pass back to one of her teammates—which Sophie intercepted for the Copperheads.

As Caitlyn trotted to her position, she stuck out her hand. Faith slapped it.

"Thanks for the backup," Caitlyn said.

"You too," Faith responded.

Faith had never played so intensely, and Coach kept her in for the rest of the match. The defense didn't allow another goal, either, and the game ended in a 2–2 tie.

After the match, Coach gave the team a few minutes of feedback and then quickly left. Faith noticed Melody trotting after him. She must have been Coach's plan B babysitter.

As Faith walked across the field toward

home, she heard a "Hey!" She stopped. Caitlyn caught up with her.

"Good match," Caitlyn said. "Sucks we didn't win, but you did good. It's like you've caught fire the past couple of games. You should think about playing club ball."

Faith shrugged. "I can't afford—"

"Hear me out a second," Caitlyn said. "My club has some scholarships. The way you're playing right now, I bet you could get one. But you'd need to play Saturdays."

Faith nodded.

"League tournaments are a great way to get seen by college scouts too" Caitlyn continued.

College. It wasn't the same thing as sharing the white cottage with Coach Berg. But in a way, it sounded even better. More real.

"I'll think about it," Faith said. "Thanks."

Caitlyn took a deep breath. "Okay. I need to show you something."

Now what? Faith thought. Caitlyn took a cell phone out of a pocket on her game bag. After showing Faith the photo, Caitlyn pressed a couple of buttons and it disappeared.

"Why?" Faith asked.

"I don't know. I suppose because I shouldn't have taken it in the first place."

It wasn't exactly an apology, but Faith was grateful anyway. She nodded.

"I need to get home."

"Yeah. See ya." Caitlyn walked toward the locker room as Faith headed in the other direction.

After taking a few steps, Faith turned and called, "Hey, Caitlyn? Um . . . if you guys are doing something Saturday night, could I, like . . ." She shrugged, too embarrassed to finish her question.

"Tag along?" Caitlyn finished for her. "Sure." She paused. "Hey, if you can wait a minute, I'll give you a ride home."

"Okay. That would be great."

about the author

M. G. HIGGINS WRITES FICTION AND NONFICTION [AS MELISSA HIGGINS] FOR CHILDREN AND YOUNG ADULTS. SHE CAN BE FOUND ONLINE AT MGHIGGINS.COM.

COUNTERATTACK

archenemy

As a defender for Fraser High, Addie used to be ready for anything. But now the biggest threat on the field is her former best friend.

the beast

When a concussion takes Alyssa out of the lineup, her rising-star teammate Becca takes over in goal. Will Alyssa heal in time for playoffs? And how far will she go to reclaim the goalie jersey?

blow out

Lacy spent the winter recovering from a knee injury that still gives her nightmares. Now Raven is going after her starting spot. Can Lacy get past her fears and play the way she used to?

offside

It might be crazy, but Faith has a crush on her coach. Can she keep her head in the game? And when Faith's frenemy Caitlyn decides that Faith's getting special treatment, will Faith become an outcast?

out of sync

Since childhood, Madison and Dayton have had soccer sync. But lately, Dayton is more interested in partying than playing soccer. Can Maddie get through to her best friend?

under pressure

Taking "performance supplements" makes Elise feel great, and lately she's been playing like a powerhouse. But will it last? How long can she keep the pills a secret?